Big thanks to Mark and
Jackie for helping me put
this together xx

pete cromer

Bushlife

This is a collection of more of my favourite Australian birds, mammals and reptiles.

Please help, protect and nurture wildlife and the environment by donating to animal conservation groups and by making conscious decisions about purchases and lifestyle choices that will lead to a brighter future.

I hope you enjoy this book filled with my art.

pete
x

Made with love by the team at

FIVE M:LE

Alex, Niki, Rocco, Graham, Jacqui, Claire, Amy, Lyndal, Emily & Jess

Five Mile,
the publishing division
of Regency Media
www.fivemile.com.au

First published 2021

A catalogue record for this book is available from the National Library of Australia

Printed in China 5 4 3 2

pete cromer

Bushlife

FiVE MiLE

Emu

Is a flightless bird. Stands up to 1.9 metres tall. Each foot has three toes. Has a big body and little wings. Its eggs are a deep blue-green colour. Has poweful legs and can run up to 50 kilometres an hour. Cannot walk backwards.

Animal group: Bird

Scientific name: *Dromaius novaehollandiae*

A young emu is called a 'chick'.

A group of emus is called a 'mob'.

Bilby

Only comes out at night. Builds underground burrows. Has poor eyesight, but excellent hearing. Pouch faces backwards to prevent dirt from entering. Uses its snout and front feet to dig for food. Lives in the desert.

Animal group: Marsupial (a mammal with a pouch)

Scientific name: *Macrotis lagotis*

A young bilby is called a 'joey'.

There is no name for a group of bilbies.
Please invent one!

Major Mitchell's Cockatoo

Nests in hollows of trees. Lives in small groups. Has pastel pink plumage and a beautifully vibrant crest. Eats seeds, fruits and nuts. Enjoys socialising with galahs.

Animal group: Bird

Scientific name: *Lophochroa leadbeateri*

A young cockatoo is called a 'chick'.

A group of cockatoos is called a 'crackle'.

Numbat

Has a long, thin and sticky tongue. Eats up to 20,000 termites a day. Is very shy. Has an excellent sense of smell. Has a long bushy tail. Lives in hollows of logs and burrows. Is active during the day. Has tiny teeth.

Animal group: Marsupial (however, does not have a proper pouch)

Scientific name: *Myrmecobius fasciatus*

A young numbat is called a 'pup'.

A group of numbats is called a 'cloud'.

Magpie

Is very intelligent. Has a beautiful flute-like bird song. Is very friendly, but known to swoop predators to defend its territory. Lives in groups of up to twenty-five. Mates for life. Can live up to 30 years in the wild.

Animal group: Bird

Scientific name: *Cracticus tibicen*

A young magpie is called a 'chick'.

A group of magpies is called a 'tiding'.

Flying Fox

Is Australia's largest flying mammal. Hangs upside-down to sleep. Is very social. Is extremely noisy. Likes to keep clean. Has excellent vision. Is vegetarian, eating nectar and fruit. Is an important pollinator of Australian trees and flowers.

Animal group: Mammal

Scientific name: *Pteropus*

A young flying fox is called a 'pup'.

A group of flying foxes is called a 'camp'.

Tawny Frogmouth

Has mottled feathers to help it camouflage, often disguising as a tree branch. Mates for life. Both parents help raise their young. Very vocal, can make purring, screaming, laughing and crying calls. Has a thick plummage to help protect itself from harsh heat and bitter colds.

Animal group: Bird

Scientific name: *Podargus strigoides*

A young tawny frogmouth is called a 'chick'.

There is no name for a group of tawny frogmouths. Please invent one!

Frilled-neck Lizard

Loves the sunshine. Eats insects. Raises its frills to scare off predators or when alarmed. Frill-span is up to 30 centimetres. Runs on its hind legs. Skin matches tree bark to help it camouflage. Lives in trees.

Animal group: Reptile

Scientific name: *Chlamydosaurus kingii*

A young lizard is called a 'hatchling'.

A group of lizards is called a 'lounge'.

Thorny Devil

Is active during the day. Walks slowly, with a rocking motion. Eats ants. Is covered in spikes to deter prey. Is able to draw water from the ground to its mouth, by using tiny grooves between its scales. Can change colour to blend into its environment. Eggs can take up to 4 months to hatch.

Animal group: Reptile

Scientific name: *Moloch horridus*

A young lizard is called a 'hatchling'.

A group of lizards is called a 'lounge'.

Blue-tongue Lizard

Mostly lives alone. Has a powerful bite. Is slow moving. Has stumpy little legs. Loves to bask in the sunshine. Will drop its tail to escape predators, and can grow it back within a year. Can live up to 30 years in the wild.

Animal group: Reptile

Scientific name: *Tiliqua scincoides*

A young lizard is called a 'hatchling'.

There is no name for a group of blue-tongue lizards. They prefer to live alone.

Lace Monitor

Is also known as a 'tree goanna'. Is an excellent climber. Has a forked tongue, like a snake. Can grow up to 2 metres in length. Eats insects, mammals, birds and eggs. Is not a fussy eater. Has long sharp claws.

Animal group: Reptile

Scientific name: *Varanus varius*

A young lizard is called a 'hatchling'.

A group of lizards is called a 'lounge'.

Quokka

Is a small wallaby. Is very friendly and curious. Lives in large groups. Has thick brown fur. Hops along the ground. Eats grass, leaves and plants. Appears to be smiling and happy, due to the shape of its mouth. Can climb trees. Is most active at night.

Animal group: Marsupial (a mammal with a pouch)

Scientific name: *Setonix brachyurus*

A young quokka is called a 'joey'.

There is no name for a group of quokkas.
Please invent one!

Southern Cassowary

Is Australia's heaviest flightless bird.
Eats fruit. Spreads seeds in its poop.
Has dangerous sharp claws. Makes
rumbling and grunting noises. The
casque, or helmet, on its head is
covered in keratin, the same material
as your fingernails.

Animal group: Bird

Scientific name: *Casuarius casuarius*

A young cassowary is called a 'chick'.

A group of cassowaries is called a 'dash'.

Eastern Quoll

Used to be known as Australia's native cat. Is covered in white spots. Fur can be either black or soft fawn. Rarely seen. Active at night. Only lives up to 4 years of age. Eats meat and fruit. Mostly lives alone, but shares its toilet sites with other quolls.

Animal group: Marsupial (a mammal with a pouch)

Scientific name: *Dasyurus viverrinus*

A young quoll is called a 'pup'.

There is no name for a group of quolls. They prefer to live alone.

Gouldian Finch

Is one of Australia's most colourful birds. Heads are coloured either red, black or yellow. Body is a rainbow of turquiose, purple, bright greens and yellow. Males are brighter than females. Nests in tree hollows. Eats seeds. Is very social.

Animal group: Bird

Scientific name: *Erythrura gouldiae*

A young gouldian finch is called a 'chick'.

A group of finches is called a 'charm'.

Dingo

Howls at night. Rarely barks. Loves meat. Is a top predator. Fur is a golden-ginger colour, with white markings. Likes to roam and hunt in groups or alone. Has lived in Australia for around 4000 years.

Animal group: Mammal

Scientific name: *Canis familiaris*

A young dingo is called a 'pup'.

A group of dingoes is called a 'pack'.

Superb Lyrebird

Mimics the calls of other birds. Can also mimic human-made sounds, like alarms and chainsaws. Spends most of its time on the ground. Seldom flies. Males have large ornate, curved tail feathers.

Animal group: Bird

Scientific name: *Menura novaehollandiae*

A young lyrebird is called a 'chick'.

A group of lyrebirds is called a 'musket'.

Little Pygmy Possum

Is the world's smallest possum. Eats nectar and pollens. Weighs only 10 grams, just a little more than a pencil. Often mistaken for a mouse. When cold, it often takes shelter in abandoned bird nests.

Animal group: Marsupial (a mammal with a pouch)

Scientific name: *Cercartetus lepidus*

A young pygmy possum is called a 'joey.'

There is no name for a group of pygmy possums. Please invent one!

pete cromer

Pete Cromer is a contemporary Australian artist based in the Colac Otway region of Victoria. Inspired by the optimistic personalities in people and wildlife, Pete's work is renowned for his signature bursts of glowing colour and beautiful textures, all reflected in his bold collages, paintings and sculptures.